Pockets

by
JENNIFER ARMSTRONG

illustrated by
MARY GRANDPRÉ

Crown Publishers, Inc. ♛ New York

Text copyright © 1998 by Jennifer M. Armstrong
Illustrations copyright © 1998 by Mary GrandPré

Published by Crown Publishers, Inc.,
a Random House company, 201 East 50th Street, New York, New York 10022

http://www.randomhouse.com/

CROWN is a trademark of Crown Publishers, Inc.

Printed in Singapore

Library of Congress Cataloging-in-Publication Data
Armstrong, Jennifer, 1961–
Pockets / by Jennifer Armstrong ; illustrated by Mary GrandPré. — 1st ed.
p. cm.
Summary: A stranger arrives at a remote village and becomes the tailor, sewing magical
embroidered scenes into the pockets of their plain clothes, which transforms
their humdrum lives forever.
[1. Tailors—Fiction. 2. Sewing—Fiction. 3. Imagination—Fiction.]
I. GrandPré, Mary, ill. II. Title.
PZ7.A73367Po 1998
[E]—dc21
97-10962

ISBN   0-517-70926-0 (trade)
0-517-70927-9 (lib. bdg.)

10 9 8 7 6 5 4 3 2 1

First Edition

j j Fic

To my mother,
who taught me to sew.
—J.A.

For Linda and Wayne.
Dreams take flight and live forever.
—M.G.

A slim schooner of a woman, driven by strong winds and a broken heart, floundered barefoot across the eastern plains until arriving at the edge of a village. Here she cast out a line and collapsed over the tiller. Some people found her in the morning, asleep in her gale-torn clothes.

Upon reviving, she either would not or could not answer their questions about her home. She had done with that, and it was sunk in the sea of her memory, never to be dredged up: The waves of the plains had rolled and tumbled her and left her stranded. The people of the village made known their cautious doubts when she asked to be taken in upon their charity, but she could work, she said, and would ask only for safe haven in return.

As the local tailor had only just died of his greed for bacon and blood sausage, the villagers asked her if she could sew. She inclined her head gravely and raised one hand in a graceful but exotic gesture. Yes, she answered, she could sew many things.

Useful things? Clothes? they pressed her. The woman closed her eyes to speak: Cotton shirts, frocks and pantaloons of bandle linen; also doublets, farthingales, damask mantuas, petticoats of drugget cloth, demi-saisons of watered silk with calamanco braiding, gowns with panne velvet godets. She knew the patterns and stitches for gigot sleeves and virago sleeves, sacque capes and pelerine capes; of fabrics she knew bengaline, brabant, abbot cloth, sarcenet, batiste, and armozeen. Her fingers were nimble with fretwork and gimped embroidery, smocking and couching, tucked seams and batuz work. She had fled from a place where such extravagance was commonplace, where travelers brought back curiosities from the corners of the globe, where the manes of horses were braided with ribbon and everyone was an inventor.

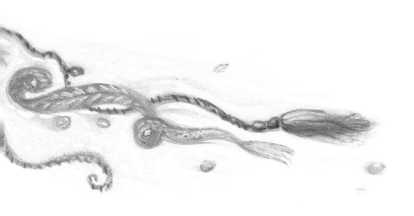

But the people of the village backed away with downcast eyes. We are plain and simple folk, and wear only the plainest, simplest habiliments: no ornamentation, no fancy work, no ribbons, no embroideries. No, no, they said with hasty, startled insistence. Out there on the plain, they had stripped themselves of distraction, the better to work. She might stay if she agreed to these terms and dressed herself in their fashion.

Because her heart was broken, the woman agreed, and she put on a dress as wan and lifeless as a November pond.

Every day she sat at the window of the tailor's boxy house, bent over her sewing. She turned out plain dresses for the women, plain shirts and trousers for the men, plain frocks and britches for the children, with stout cloth, sturdy seams, and careful hems.

There came a day, however, when the sight of so many plain and unadorned clothes caused her heart a new kind of pain. True, it beat strong under the breast of her simple dress, but it took no joy in its routine and did not expect to take any in the future. Hour after hour on this particular day, the woman sat at the window, her needle quiet in her lap, her thimble forgotten under the chair where it had rolled, while she gazed mutinously at the unchanging landscape.

The pieces of gray cloth by her side were meant for a dress for herself, and the sight of it made her long for sunny ports. So she took her bearings, and turned the pockets inside out. Then she proceeded to embroider them.

Her needle dipped and darted through the fabric, steering itself into a pattern of the sea lion and the albatross, manatees, corals, and blue-finned fishes. She sewed barkentines, ships of the line, brigs, dhows, triremes, and caravels; cays, lagoons, and scalloped beaches; the astrolabe, the sextant, and the binnacle, each in perfect miniature, her stitches straining ahead against the current and her eyes narrowed on the horizon

When she had done, and turned the pockets to the inside again, she slipped her hands into them. She smiled as her fingers read the charts inside. With pockets such as these, she could bear to be becalmed on the plains.

All of her own clothes she now appointed in this way. Her pockets contained hidden oceans and harbors, spangled and knobbed with the buttons, shells, silk braids, and tassels she sent for. When she wasn't sewing, she stood at her window, with her hands in her pockets, and navigated.

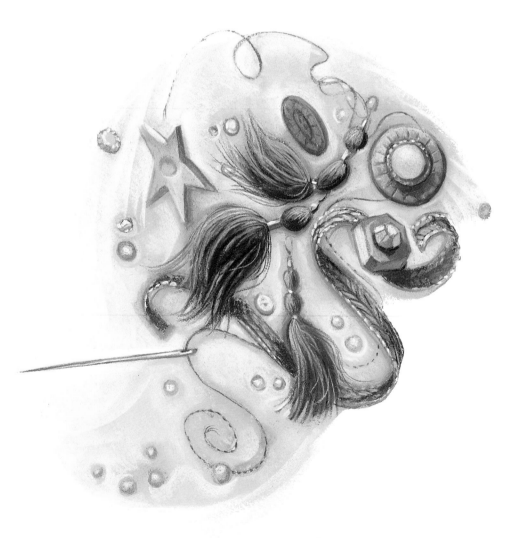

For some time, she was content to keep her adventuring confined to the pockets of her own dresses. But as she continued to sew the ugly, land-locked clothes for the people of the village, she pitied her neighbors.

These people plied a steady course from birth to death, toiling under all weathers, seldom looking to the sky but to judge how many hours of work they might still get in before the sun slipped away. The plains around them swallowed color and drowned it, and the village itself drifted sadly, a sunless island.

On the day after a soaking rain, the mayor's wife was seen wearing a new gray dress, standing rigid in the doorway of her house, with her hands in her pockets. Shortly afterward, a passing child heard her sobbing wildly upstairs and ran for the mayor. That good man and the doctor patted her shoulder to no avail. They did not suspect that she had been assailed by visions of the golden towers of Constantinople, with its sweaty crowds roaring in the hippodrome, and the dolphins leaping beside the red-hulled caiques in the Sea of Marmara, and the markets full of pomegranates and murder.

For several days the mayor's wife was inconsolable, but then awakened from a long, heavy, dream-tossed sleep and began to collect the small flowers that grew in the cracks of the stone walls. She put these in jars on the windowsills and taught herself to sing.

One evening, laughter echoed from the blacksmith's shop, ringing out with the blows of hammer on anvil.

Beneath his leather apron the smith wore new pants, whose pockets had surrounded him with the high-masted forests of Stavanger, Vigrestad, and Sandnes on the Rogaland coast of Norway, where dragon-prowed ships cut through fjords turned silver with herring. The Viking fire that made the forge glow red that evening caused mothers to pull their daughters close, and made young men pause in their work, smell the air, and whisper words like *hard alee, halyard, tropic of Cancer.*

And the husband and wife who never spoke to one another suddenly found, each in the other, charms and delights never before noticed. When she looked at him, she saw a buccaneer holding pink shells, black pearls, and a sword; when he looked at her, he begged to be tied to the mast lest he die of her beauty.

The seamstress worked on and on under full sail through all the watches. She refreshed herself by tracing her finger along the profiles of sailors, the notation of sea-song, and the outlines of the hemispheres that filled her pockets. Soon, the entire village stopped working at the weary, endless tasks for long passages of time. Instead of stooping to the plow and the loom, sweating at washtubs and ovens, and hardening their hands carrying burdens from one place to another, they took moments out to stand singly or in pairs, squinting at far horizons in their treasure-laden clothes.

Flags began to appear on rooftops, snapping in the wind, and both men and women spoke of places whose latitude and longitude filled their mouths with honey and salt. Dances were held in the courtyards of houses newly painted in crimson, azure, and gold. Girls discussed poetics, men developed the taste for pies, pastries, and tarts, women studied maps with their sons, and everyone learned the names of the stars.

And then, when the entire village resembled
nothing so much as a bounding caravel making for
home before a strong wind, its crew looking out for
landfall and filled with stories of its travels, the
young woman,

    whose heart was now complete again,
      turned her compass
        toward her old home,
          and cast off.